This book belongs to:

Jayda

Retold by Monica Hughes
Illustrated by Adrienne Salgado

Reading consultants: Betty Root and Monica Hughes

This edition published by Parragon in 2010

Parragon
Queen Street House
4 Queen Street
Bath BA1 1HE, UK

ISBN 978-1-4454-1212-2

Printed in China

Rapunzel

Bath · New York · Singapore · Hong Kong · Cologne · Delhi · Melbourne

Helping your child to read

These books are closely linked to recognized learning strategies. Their vocabulary has been carefully selected from the word lists recommended by educational experts.

Read the story
Read the story
to your child
a few times.

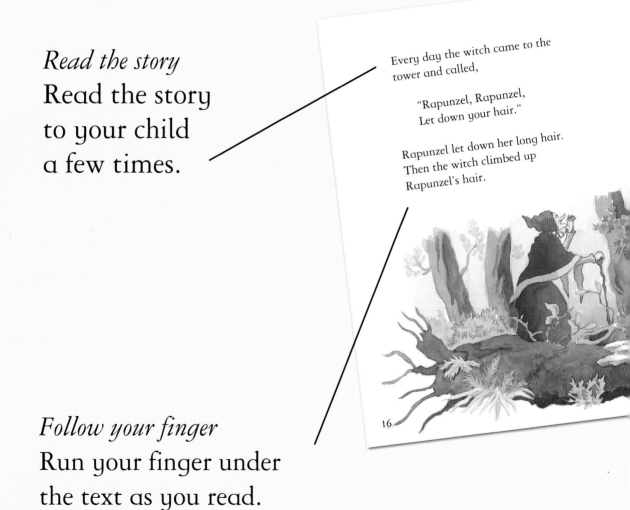

Every day the witch came to the tower and called,

"Rapunzel, Rapunzel,
Let down your hair."

Rapunzel let down her long hair.
Then the witch climbed up
Rapunzel's hair.

16

Follow your finger
Run your finger under
the text as you read.
Your child will soon begin to
follow the words with you.

Look at the pictures
Talk about the pictures. They will help your child to understand the story.

"Rapunzel, Rapunzel, Let down your hair."

17

Give it a try
Let your child try reading the large type on each right-hand page. It repeats a line from the story.

Join in
When your child is ready, encourage him or her to join in with the main story text. Shared reading is the first step to reading alone.

Once there was a man and his wife.
The wife was going to have a baby.
But she was sick.
A witch lived next door.
The witch had a garden.
It was full of rapunzel plants.
The leaves were good to eat.

The witch had a garden.

"I must eat rapunzel leaves or I will
die," said the wife.

So the man went into the witch's
garden.

The man picked the leaves.

His wife ate the leaves, and she did
not die.

The man picked the leaves every day.

The man picked the leaves.

One day the witch saw him.
"Why are you stealing my leaves?"
she said.
"My wife must eat them or she will
die," said the man.
"You can have my leaves," said
the witch, "but you must give me
your baby."

Soon the baby was born.
The baby was called Rapunzel.
The man gave the baby to the witch.

He gave the baby to the witch.

Soon Rapunzel grew into a beautiful girl
with long, long hair.
The witch took Rapunzel to a tower.
The tower had one window.
But there was no door.
Rapunzel lived alone in the tower.
Every day she sat at the window singing.

The witch took Rapunzel
to a tower.

Every day the witch came to the
tower and called,

"Rapunzel, Rapunzel,
Let down your hair."

Rapunzel let down her long hair.
Then the witch climbed up
Rapunzel's hair.

"Rapunzel, Rapunzel,
Let down your hair."

One day a prince came by.
He heard Rapunzel singing.
He wanted to get into the tower.
But there was no door.

Then the prince saw the witch.
He heard her say,

"Rapunzel, Rapunzel,
Let down your hair."

He saw her climb up Rapunzel's hair.

When the witch went away, the
prince said,

"Rapunzel, Rapunzel,
Let down your hair."

The prince climbed up Rapunzel's hair.

One day a prince came by.

Every time the witch went away, the
prince came to see Rapunzel.

One day Rapunzel told the witch about
the prince.
The witch was very angry.
"I will cut off your hair," said the
witch.
The witch cut off Rapunzel's hair.
Then the witch sent Rapunzel away.

"I will cut off your hair," said
the witch.

The prince came to the tower.
He did not hear Rapunzel singing.
But he said,

"Rapunzel, Rapunzel,
Let down your hair."

The witch let down Rapunzel's hair.
The prince climbed up Rapunzel's hair.

The witch let down Rapunzel's hair.

When the prince got to the window
he saw the witch.
The witch was very angry.
She let go of Rapunzel's hair.
The prince fell down.
He fell into a thorn bush.
The thorns went in his eyes, and
he could not see.

The prince fell down.

The prince walked for days.
Then he heard someone singing.
It was Rapunzel!
The prince told her about the witch.
Rapunzel cried.
Her tears fell into the prince's eyes.
They washed away the thorns.
The prince could see!

The prince and Rapunzel were married,
and they all lived happily ever after.

The prince and Rapunzel were married.

Look back in your book.
Can you read these words?

Rapunzel

witch

prince

tower

baby

Can you answer these questions?

Who gave the baby
to the witch?

Where did Rapunzel live?

Who cut off
Rapunzel's hair?